BOARD OF EDUCATION
BOWLING GREEN, OHIO

CADMUS BOOKS

D1621694

BIG RED BARN

By Margaret Wise Brown

Illustrated by Rosella Hartman

"In the Big Red Barn, in the great green field, there was a pink pig who was learning to squeal. There was a great big horse, and a very little horse, and on every barn there is a weathervane, of course — A golden flying horse."

All these and more this distinguished story teller writes about in the red barn.

K

Classification and Dewey Decimal: Easy (E)

About the Author:

MARGARET WISE BROWN liked boys and girls. She liked to talk to them about things that interested them. She put these into more than a hundred books young people have read and loved — *The Little Farmer, The Runaway Bunny, Sneakers, Young Kangaroo, Big Red Barn,* and others. Miss Brown came from a Virginia family but spent most of her life in New York and Europe. She was educated in Virginia, New England and Switzerland, and for some time was an editor of children's books. Young children, especially, not only love to read Miss Brown's books, but often act them out, and many take them to bed at night. Under the name of Golden MacDonald she wrote *The Little Island*. The illustrations were by Leonard Weisgard and was awarded the Caldecott Medal in 1947.

About the Illustrator:

ROSELLA HARTMAN is a serious artist having had seven one-man shows in New York City. She studied at Chicago Art Institute and the Art Students League in New York, receiving several fellowships and grants. She has had exhibitions at the Metropolitan, Chicago Art Institute, Corcoran Gallery in Washington, and is represented in many other famous collections. The illustrations for this book are the only ones she has done for children.

big red barn

By Margaret Wise Brown

Illustrated by Rosella Hartman

1961 FIRST CADMUS EDITION
THIS SPECIAL EDITION IS PUBLISHED BY ARRANGEMENT WITH
THE PUBLISHERS OF THE REGULAR EDITION
WILLIAM R. SCOTT, INC.
BY
E. M. HALE AND COMPANY
EAU CLAIRE, WISCONSIN

MLVI BY WILLIAM R. SCOTT, INC. MADE IN U.S.A. LIBRARY OF CONGRESS CATALOG CARD NUMBER 56-5404.

By the big red barn
In the great green field,

There was a pink pig
Who was learning to squeal.

There was a great big horse
And a very little horse.

And on every barn
There is a weathervane, of course—
A golden flying horse.

There was a big pile of hay
And a little pile of hay,
And that is where the children would play.
But in this story the children are away,
And only the animals are here today.

The sheep and the donkey
And the geese and the goats
Were making funny noises
Out of their throats.

An old scarecrow
Was leaning on his hoe.
And a field mouse was born
In a field of corn.

Cock-a-doodle-dooooo!
In the barn there was a rooster
And a pigeon, too.
And a big white hen
Standing on one leg.
And under the hen was a quiet egg.

There was a bantam rooster
And a little bantam hen
With a big clutch of eggs,
If you can count to ten.

Cock-a-doodle-doo!

Moooooooooo! Moo!
A big brown cow

And a little brown cow
Both ate their dinner
Of hay from the mow.

There was an old black cat,
Meow! Meow!
And a tiger tom cat,
Yeow! Yeow!

And an old red dog,
Bow! Wow!
With some little puppy dogs
All round and warm.

And they all lived together
In the big red barn.
And they played all day
In the grass and in the hay.

Until the sun went down
In the great green field.

The big cow lowed,
The little pig squealed,

The horses stomped in the sweet warm hay,
And the little donkey gave one last bray.

The little black bats flew away
Out of the barn at the end of the day.
The hens were sleeping on their nests.
Even the roosters took a rest.

And the geese and the goats
Made no more noises with their throats.

And there they were all night long
Sound asleep in the big red barn.
And only the mice were left to play,
Rustling and squeaking in the hay.

The moon sailed high
In the dark night sky.

Beyond the house
Where the children slept,
The tiger cat
Crept home to his kittens
In the big red barn.

But out in the field
The old scarecrow
Still leaned on his hoe.

PROPERTY OF
MILTON SCHOOL